Rapunzel

This edition first published in 2007 by
Sea-to-Sea Publications
1980 Lookout Drive
North Mankato
Minnesota 56003

Printed in China

Library of Congress Cataloging-in-Publication Data
Robinson, Hilary, 1962-
  Rapunzel / by Hilary Robinson.
    p. cm. -- (First fairy tales)
  Summary: A simplified version of the tale in which Rapunzel, who has long golden
hair, is kept imprisoned in a lonely tower by a witch.
  ISBN-13: 978-1-59771-076-3
    [1. Fairy tales. 2. Folklore- -Germany. 3. Hair- -Folklore.] I. Rapunzel. English. II.
Title. III. Series.

PZ8.R565Rap 2006
398.2--dc22
[E]
                                                                            2005057546

9 8 7 6 5 4 3 2

Published by arrangement with the Watts Publishing Group Ltd, London

Series Editor: Jackie Hamley
Series Advisor: Linda Gambrell, Dr. Barrie Wade
Series Designer: Peter Scoulding

For Andrew – H.R.

For Emilie – M.I.

Rapunzel

Retold by Hilary Robinson

Illustrated by Martin Impey

SEA-TO-SEA
Mankato Collingwood London

Once upon a time, there was a beautiful girl with long, golden hair.

Her name was Rapunzel.
A wicked witch hid her
in a tower with no door.

Rapunzel could not escape.
She was so bored that she
sang all day long.

To get into the tower the witch would cry:

Rapunzel, Rapunzel,
let down your hair!

Then she would climb up
Rapunzel's long hair.

One day a prince rode by

He heard Rapunzel singing
and fell in love with her.

He watched how the witch climbed into the tower.

Later, he called:

Rapunzel, Rapunzel,
let down your hair!

13

The prince climbed into the tower. Rapunzel soon fell in love with him. They planned her escape.

Rapunzel made a ladder from some silk the prince had brought her.

Soon she would be able
to climb out of the tower.

But when the witch next
came to see her, Rapunzel
made a big mistake.

She cried: "Why are you
so much heavier than
the prince?"

The witch was furious.

She cut off Rapunzel's hair.

Then she hid her in
the woods.

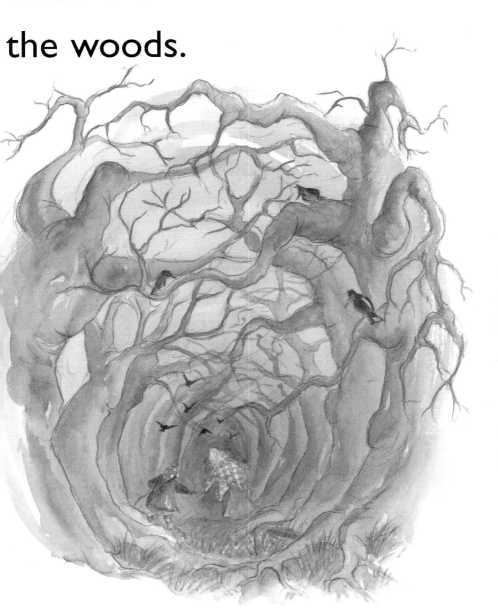

Later, the prince rode to the tower. He called:

Rapunzel, Rapunzel, let down your hair!

But when he climbed up
he saw...

…the angry witch! "Away!" she cried and pushed him onto the thorns below.

The prince's eyes were scratched by the thorns. He couldn't see anymore.

For two years he was lost in the woods.

Then, one day, he heard
beautiful singing.
"Rapunzel!" he cried.

Rapunzel's tears of joy
helped the prince to
see again.

The prince led Rapunzel to his palace where they lived happily ever after.

978-1-59771-071-8

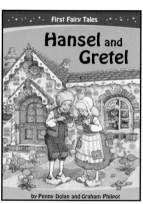

978-1-59771-075-6

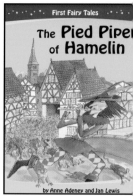

978-1-59771-072-5

978-1-59771-076-3

978-1-59771-073-2

978-1-59771-074-9